# rainbow

# A DAY AT THE SEASIDE

Written by Clive Hopwood
Illustrated by Paul Crompton

Copyright © 1989 Thames Television Plc.
All rights reserved.
Published in Great Britain by World International Publishing Limited,
An Egmont Company, Egmont House, P.O. Box 111, Great Ducie Street, Manchester M60 3BL.
Printed in Germany. ISBN 7235 1355 4
4th Reprint

George is very excited. He wakes up early. He wakes up Bungle and Zippy too. They are just as excited. Today is a special day.

They all look out of the window.
"The sun is shining," says
George.
"The sky is blue," says Bungle.
"What a perfect day," says
Zippy.

They go to wake up Geoffrey. His bed is empty. He is not there.

They find him in the kitchen. He is making breakfast.

"We're all up early," says Geoffrey. "That's good. We don't want to waste this sunshine. Go and wash and get dressed."

In no time at all George, Bungle and Zippy are ready for their breakfast.

"Isn't it exciting?" says George. "A day at the seaside!"

"Well, don't be too excited to eat your breakfast," says Geoffrey. "We all need something inside us for the journey."

George, Zippy, Bungle and Geoffrey eat up their breakfast.

They wash up the breakfast things. They remember their swimming costumes and some towels.

"Is everyone ready?" asks Geoffrey. They all nod. "Then off we go to the seaside."

They catch the bus to the railway station. George, Bungle and Zippy look out of the windows as they go along.

"We're going ever so fast," says George.

Soon it is their stop. The bus slows down and stops outside the railway station.

"Don't forget your things," says Geoffrey as they get off.

Geoffrey takes them to the ticket office. He buys four tickets.

The railway station is busy. Trains are coming and going all the time.

George is worried. "Where do we go?" he asks. "There are so many people and so many trains."
"Don't worry, George," says Geoffrey. "Stay close to me."

Geoffrey has a timetable. "Our train leaves in ten minutes," says Geoffrey. "Now we have to find which platform the train is on."

They go and look at a big noticeboard.

On the board are all the times of the trains. It tells them which platforms the trains leave from. And it tells them where the trains are going.

Bungle finds the place they are going to. Zippy finds the time of their train. George finds the platform number.

"It leaves from Platform 2," he says.

Soon they are on the train.
"It's moving," says Bungle. Sure
enough the train is starting to move.
It leaves the station. They are on
their way.

The train speeds along. They look out of the windows.

"This train goes much faster than the bus," says George. "Isn't it exciting?"

Everyone agrees.

Before long they arrive at the seaside.

They head for the beach. "Wait for me," says Geoffrey. "Don't go in the water without me."

"The water's colder than the sunshine," says Bungle.

"Yes, but it's all right once you're in," says Zippy. "You soon get used to it."

They all enjoy going in the water.
They play splashing games. Bungle
finds some seaweed and pretends
to be a monster. It is all great fun.

When everyone is dry they go for a walk along the beach. They try and walk as close to the water as they can without getting wet. It isn't easy!

Bungle is looking for pretty shells.

George is looking for pieces of driftwood.

Zippy is looking for stones.

Geoffrey puts them all in his bag.

"Can we have an ice-cream please, Geoffrey?" asks Zippy. "I'm hungry."

Geoffrey smiles. "A very special ice-cream," he says. "And that's not all. Come on!"

Geoffrey takes them to a cafe. He orders fish and chips for each of them. Then as a special treat they each have an ice-cream in a tall glass.

Soon it is time to catch the train
home. They are all tired but happy.
"What a lovely day at the
seaside," say Zippy, George and
Bungle. "Thank you, Geoffrey."
But Geoffrey is fast asleep!